HIRO'S QUEST

Enemy Rising

Enemy Rising

by Tracey West

Illustrated by Craig Phillips

Scholastic Inc.

New York   Toronto   London   Auckland   Sydney
Mexico City   New Delhi   Hong Kong   Buenos Aires

For my editor, Jenne Abramowitz,

whose creative ideas gave life to Hiro and his journey

— T. W.

ISBN-13: 978-0-545-16288-3
ISBN-10: 0-545-16288-2

12 11 10 9 8 7 6 5 4 3 2 1   9 10 11 12 13 14/0

Printed in the U.S.A.
First printing, September 2009
Book design by Jennifer Rinaldi Windau

Chapter One

"One . . . two . . . three!"

Hiro Hinata sprang up on his toes, launching himself into the air. He did a backflip, landing lightly on the damp ground. Without stopping, he did another backflip, and another. Then he jumped into the air a fourth time. His sandals hit the earth, but he slipped, landing on his back.

"Rats," Hiro muttered. The spring rains had fallen again last night, leaving the ground muddy. He jumped to his feet, determined to try again.

His brother Kenta could do five backflips in a row without stopping. Hiro never made it past three, no matter how hard he tried. He brushed the mud off of his brown trousers and looked at the sky.

It was a good day for training. The rain had passed, and now the sky above was a brilliant shade of blue. The hilly peaks of the mountains rose up all around Hiro to catch the rays of the sun. The small, simple houses of Hissori Village were tucked into the mountainsides wherever they could fit.

A long, snaking path led from the main village down to the small grassy field used for ninja training. Hiro saw his teacher, Mr. Sato, step off of the path. Mr. Sato walked slowly, leaning on his tall walking stick. His long white beard shone like the moon against his dark gray tunic. As Mr. Sato got closer, Hiro could see a maze of lines etched deeply into his wrinkled face.

"Good morning, Hiro. You are very early today."

Hiro bowed deeply at the waist to show respect for his teacher.

"Good morning, *sensei*," Hiro said. "I got here before the sun came up. I don't want to miss anything today."

Mr. Sato had said they would be learning animal transformations this week. Hiro was afraid to say anything out loud, in case the sensei had changed his mind.

Hiro had been studying the ninja arts since he could walk. Back then, he could only take a few steps on a balance beam before he fell off. Now he could balance on a log bobbing on the bouncing waves of the village stream for hours, all thanks to his training.

His mom, dad, and two older brothers were all skilled ninja. The Hinata family were the protectors of their mountain village. Hiro had studied with his parents when he was younger, but Mr. Sato had taken over the training when he turned six.

Hiro worked hard to catch up to his family. He

could run fast but still could not beat his father in a race. He could kick high, but his oldest brother, Kazuki, could kick higher. His mother could walk across a creaky floor without making a sound, but Hiro always ended up making a loud squeak.

Hiro was so focused on being as skilled as his family that he sometimes forgot the things he was very good at. He could climb faster and higher than his brothers and parents. But there was one thing Hiro couldn't do, and that bothered Hiro most of all. When ninja turned ten or eleven, they could tap in to the animal spirit inside them and transform at will. Hiro had no idea how do to that. Mr. Sato hadn't taught them how—yet.

"It's animal day! It's animal day!"

Hiro's friend Yoshi bounded across the field. He was a full head shorter than Hiro, with silvery-white hair and bright blue eyes. His face was flushed with excitement when he reached Hiro and Mr. Sato.

"Can we start now?" Yoshi asked.

Mr. Sato bowed. "Good morning, Yoshi."

Yoshi's face colored again. Hiro knew his friend hadn't meant to be rude. Yoshi just got impatient sometimes.

Yoshi bowed. "Sorry, sensei. Good morning." He paused. "So when are we starting?"

"As you know, we are waiting for one more student," Mr. Sato replied.

"Aya," Yoshi said, tapping his foot. "She'd better not be late."

"Actually, I'm early."

Hiro jumped at the sound of Aya's voice. Calm, cool Aya always moved as silently as falling snow. She stepped between the two boys and bowed to Mr. Sato.

"Good morning, sensei."

The teacher returned the greeting. "You are all early today. That is a good thing." He nodded to them. "Please center your energies."

The three students formed a line, standing a few feet apart. Hiro closed his eyes and pressed his palms together, pointing his fingers toward the sky. He took a deep breath.

Mr. Sato began all of their lessons this way. Hiro waited for the sound of the teacher's voice to open his eyes. This morning, he felt as impatient as Yoshi.

Hiro slowly opened one eye. Mr. Sato stood as still as a statue in front of him. Hiro glanced at Aya next to him. She was taller than Hiro, with sleek, straight black hair. Her eyes were peacefully closed, but when they were open, they were the same emerald green color as her tunic. Next to her, Yoshi fidgeted, his right leg jiggling up and down.

"Very good," Mr. Sato said. Hiro quickly faced forward. "Now, as I promised, this week we will study animal transformation."

"Yes!" Yoshi cried. "So how do we start? I'm guessing we need to memorize a series of fighting moves."

"More likely a charm or a spell," Aya added.

"Let Mr. Sato talk!" Hiro blurted out. He was so

excited he felt like doing another backflip. They were finally going to learn how to transform!

"To transform into your animal spirit, close your eyes," Mr. Sato began.

All three students obeyed. They waited for Mr. Sato to speak again, but the teacher was silent.

"Now what?" Yoshi asked.

"Now you must connect to the spirit inside you," Mr. Sato explained. "You and your animal spirit are one and the same. You have the same bones, the same skin, the same heart. To transform, you must only will yourself to do so."

Hiro closed his eyes and tried to concentrate, but he couldn't control his thoughts.

One and the same. Hiro had often wondered what animal spirit was hidden inside him. Maybe a tiger, like his father? But his dad was quiet, powerful, and strong. Hiro didn't feel powerful or strong. Kazuki's spirit was a big bear, which matched his big body and rough personality perfectly. But Hiro wasn't big. He was wiry, like his brother Kenta. Maybe he would turn into a wolf, like Kenta did.

Hiro wondered if Aya and Yoshi were doing any better than he was. Then he heard Aya's voice and opened his eyes.

"Are you sure there isn't a charm?" Aya asked. "We could go look at the books in the temple."

"Try calling out to the spirit," Mr. Sato suggested. "If you are ready, it will come."

"But we don't even know what kind of animal our spirit is," Hiro said. "How can we call out to something if we don't even know what it is?"

"Ah, but you do know," Mr. Sato replied. "Your animal spirit shines in your human form. The traits of your animal appear in your own likes and dislikes, your strengths and weaknesses. Why, I can see your animals just by looking at you."

"So can't you just tell us?" Yoshi asked.

The old man's eyes twinkled. "It does not work that way. You must do this yourself. Now concentrate."

Hiro closed his eyes again. He had seen his

parents and brothers transform in an instant. They made it look so easy. He hoped it would be easy for him, too.

Hey there, animal spirit, Hiro called out with his mind. *It's Hiro. Are you there?*

Nothing happened. Hiro tried again. He scrunched up all of the muscles in his face, concentrating as hard as he could, but that didn't work.

He tried to picture his animal spirit, but he still had no idea what he might be. Even though he was built like Kenta, he didn't feel like a wolf. Maybe he was something fierce, too. Some kind of mountain lion, maybe . . .

Hiro concentrated and concentrated. He stood there for a long time—how long, he wasn't sure—when he heard Yoshi cry out.

"I'm doing it!"

Hiro opened his eyes in time to see silvery-white hair sprouting all over Yoshi's body. His friend got shorter and shorter, but his ears got longer and longer.

Now a rabbit was hopping up and down in front

of him. Hiro blinked. Yoshi had transformed into a rabbit!

Yoshi stood on his hind legs and started waving his arms about. "Look at me! Karate rabbit!"

"Quiet!" Aya said. Her voice sounded strange. "I'm concentrating."

Hiro gasped. Shiny green scales covered Aya's face and arms. She was turning into some kind of reptile. But she hadn't fully transformed yet.

He stared at his friend, feeling frustrated and amazed at the same time. Aya and Yoshi had both found their animal spirits. Why couldn't he?

Chapter Two

"How do you do it?" Hiro asked. He was walking up the steep path that led back to the village. Aya walked by his side, and Yoshi raced up ahead of both of them. "Is there some kind of trick?"

Aya shook her head. "No, Mr. Sato was right. I just thought about what kind of animal spirit might be inside me. I tried to think of things I'm best at, and then I just knew I was a snake. Once I felt it, it just happened."

"But it can't be that simple!" Hiro protested. "I tried that."

Hiro had tried to transform for hours. Both Aya and Yoshi had learned to transform from human to animal and back again. Yoshi had found that as a rabbit, he was faster than he ever could be in his human form. Aya was more agile in snake form, with a pair of fangs to boot. Hiro was exhausted, and had nothing to show for it.

Aya shrugged. "I don't know what to say. That's how I did it. Didn't you get any kind of animal feeling at all?"

Hiro shook his head. "Nothing. I have no idea what my animal spirit might be."

Aya nodded to Yoshi, who practically bounced as he made his way up the trail. "I guess with some people, the animal part of them is easy to figure out. I wouldn't be surprised if he was born with a fluffy tail."

Hiro laughed. "You're right. And you've always been able to move silently, like a snake. But I don't

feel like any animal at all." He shook his head.
"Maybe I'll never transform."

"Yes, you will," Aya said. She sounded certain.
"Try thinking of things you're good at, like I did.
You know you're a great climber."

Hiro tried to think of animals that could climb
well. He could think of only one. "So I guess there's
a mountain goat inside me, then. I'll really strike
fear into the hearts of my enemies now."

Aya smiled. "I could be wrong, but I don't think
there's a goat inside you," she said. "And even if
there is, I'm sure it's a totally amazing goat."

"See you tomorrow!" Yoshi called from the trail
above. He waved and hurried along the path that
led to his house.

Hiro and Aya soon reached Aya's house, just off
the main trail.

"Good-bye, Hiro," she said. "I'm sure tomorrow
will be better."

"I hope so," Hiro muttered as he slowly made his
way up the trail.

Hiro was in no hurry to get home. He had told his whole family that Mr. Sato was teaching animal transformation today, and they would want to hear all about it. His brothers would tease him for sure when they found out he couldn't do it.

Hiro rounded a bend and came upon Mr. Sato's house. A rickety old fence surrounded a small yard for Mr. Sato's brown chickens. A red rooster strutted among them with his chest puffed out.

With my luck, I'll transform into a chicken, Hiro thought glumly. *Kazuki will probably pluck out my feathers and make a pillow out of them.*

He paused in front of a rain barrel just outside the fence and peered inside. His dim reflection stared back at him.

What animal do I look like? Hiro wondered. He stared for a moment, but all he could see was the same old face he saw every morning when he brushed his teeth. His eyes were golden brown, the same color as his dad's. His nose wasn't too small or too big. And his thick hair was streaked with red and gold. It was always a little bit messy.

Maybe I'm a lion? Hiro thought hopefully. He closed his eyes, searching for the inner bravery of a lion, but nothing came to him.

"Still training, Hiro?"

Hiro opened his eyes to see Mr. Sato behind the fence, feeding his chickens. He was certain his teacher had been way behind him on the path. How had he reached his home so quickly?

"Training all the time is no good, Hiro," Mr. Sato cautioned. "You need to play a little, too."

"Yes, sensei," Hiro replied, feeling embarrassed as he hurried home. There was no point in putting off facing his family.

When he entered the house, his mother was placing steaming bowls of food on the dining table. Kenta, Kazuki, and his father, Yuto, were already seated. Yuto's reddish hair was bushy, like Hiro's, but cropped close to his head.

"How did it go today, Hiro?" Yuto asked. "Did you transform?"

Hiro took a seat across from Kazuki. He wasn't sure what to say.

"I'll bet he turned into a slug," Kenta said, grinning. "Nice and slow, and never able to beat me in a race. Eh, little brother?"

Hiro knew he was just teasing, but it only made him feel worse.

Across the table, Kazuki was piling noodles into his bowl. "I'd bet he turned into a skunk. Because he stinks! Get it? Ha!"

Kazuki laughed at his own joke. At seventeen, he was taller than each of his parents and as wide as both of them together.

"I didn't transform into anything," Hiro said quietly. He looked down at the table.

Hiro's mom, Rino, gracefully slipped into her seat. Her blue hair was neatly tied in a bun at the nape of her neck.

"It was only your first day, Hiro," she said.

"But isn't he, like, eleven?" Kazuki asked. "I was turning into a bear before I was ten!"

"You were born a bear," Rino said, giving her son a warning glance. "This conversation is over. We have more important things to talk about. Now pass the rice to your brother, Kazuki."

Hiro gave his mom a small, grateful smile. He took the bowl from Kazuki. All that was left was one spoonful. Hiro sighed but didn't say anything. There was no point in arguing with Kazuki.

"So what's the news?" Kenta asked eagerly. Fifteen-year-old Kenta was tall and fit, with the same blue-gray eyes as his mom and Kazuki. His blue hair was short on the sides and spiked on top.

"Fujita is back," Yuto answered. Hiro put down his chopsticks.

Like every child in the kingdom of Kenkoro, Hiro had heard stories about Fujita since he could remember. The evil ninja was said to have mysterious powers. Some said he could become completely invisible. Others said he could stop time. No ninja who had faced Fujita had lived to talk about it—that's what the stories said, anyway.

Fujita lived in Hiro's imagination like the villain in a fairy tale. But whatever his powers were, the ninja was very real. He and his men had been ransacking villages all over the countryside.

"He struck again last night, not far from here," Yuto said. "Kazuki and I will stand guard tonight at the village tower."

"Dad, what does he want?" Hiro asked.

"Nobody knows for sure," Yuto replied. "But he seems to be searching for something."

"Do you really think he'll come here?" Hiro asked.

"If he comes here, he'll have to get past me," Kazuki boasted. "That's not going to happen."

"Be careful, Kazuki." Rino gave her son a stern look. "Fujita is more dangerous than you know."

That night, Hiro lay in bed in the room he shared with his brothers. Kenta was out with his friends and wouldn't be home until after Hiro was asleep, and Kazuki was on guard duty. The threat of Fujita made Hiro nervous, but there was one good thing about it. Without Kazuki's snoring, he'd be sure to get a good night's sleep.

Exhausted from his training, Hiro fell asleep quickly. He was dreaming of rabbits when the clanging of a loud bell jerked him from his sleep.

Hiro sat up in bed, his heart pounding. His father had sounded the village alarm. That could mean only one thing.

Fujita was here!

Chapter Three

Hiro slipped on a tunic and ran to Kenta's bed. He shook his brother awake.

"Kenta, the alarm!" Hiro cried.

Kenta jumped up. He grabbed a shirt from a pile of clothes on the floor and raced out the door ahead of Hiro. They found their mother by the front door, ready to go. The sound of the alarm bells had stopped, and all was quiet.

"Where should we go?" Hiro asked. Yuto and

Kazuki must have seen Fujita and his men enter the village. Had they attacked the tower?

Rino held up a finger. "Listen."

Ko-ke-kok-ko-o! Ko-ke-kok-ko-o!

Hiro immediately recognized the sound of the rooster's cry. "Mr. Sato!"

Before his mother could stop him, Hiro ran down the trail as quickly as he could. Old Mr. Sato was a good teacher, but there was no way he could defend himself against an evil ninja and a gang of thugs.

He reached Mr. Sato's house and ran through the open front door, breathless. Mr. Sato was standing on top of a table, fighting off five ninja dressed in black. A strip of black fabric covered the bottom half of each ninja's face. They were using every trick they knew to subdue old Mr. Sato. But to Hiro's surprise, his teacher looked strong. As the ninja charged him, he beat them back one by one with his walking stick. *WHACK! WHACK!*

Then one of the ninja dove at Mr. Sato's feet and

grabbed him by the ankles. He pulled the old man down, and Mr. Sato tumbled off of the table.

Hiro moved to help, but Kenta bounded through the door, accidentally knocking down his little brother. He charged at the ninja nearest Mr. Sato and leveled him with one swift, strong kick.

Rino flew through the door next, and immediately grabbed the nearest ninja and flipped him over as easily as if he were a bag of rice. Then she reached down and helped Mr. Sato to his feet.

Hiro stood up, not sure what to do. He had trained to be a ninja for years, but he had never been in a real battle before. Everything was happening so fast.

The sound of a loud growl caused Hiro to turn his head. A big brown bear stood on two legs just outside the doorway. It tried to enter but came to a sudden stop at the threshold. The animal transformed into Hiro's brother Kazuki. He looked confused for a moment, and then he charged inside.

Kazuki picked up one of the ninja and tossed him

onto a nearby chair, splintering it. Two of the ninja had Kenta cornered against the wall. Hiro watched in amazement as Mr. Sato somersaulted across the table and landed between the two thugs. He reached out and delivered an open-palm blow to each one at the same time, sending them flying.

"I have them!"

One of the ninja held up two rolled-up scrolls of paper. He darted toward the front door, running right past Hiro.

Hiro acted without thinking. He knew the scrolls must be important. He jumped up and grabbed one of the ceiling beams, swinging himself toward the ninja. He reached out and grabbed at the scrolls. A few scraps of thin paper tore off in his hand, but the ninja carrying them didn't even notice. He raced off toward a stand of pines.

"He's getting away!" Hiro shouted.

The remaining four ninja charged past Hiro. Rino, Kenta, and Kazuki chased after them, but they didn't get far.

"Let them go," Mr. Sato said firmly. "This is not the time to fight Fujita." He nodded into the darkness.

Hiro followed his gaze. A tall, dark figure emerged from the trees. It was impossible to make out his face in the dark, but Fujita's eyes glowed red. He laughed, and Hiro had never heard such a sinister sound. A chill of fear crept through his body.

The real Fujita was different from the villain he had heard about in stories.

He was much, much scarier.

Chapter Four

Fujita and his men disappeared into the darkness as Hiro's father ran up to Mr. Sato's house.

"Is everyone all right?" Yuto asked. "Three men attacked us at the watchtower. I sent Kazuki ahead and fought them off."

"Nobody is hurt," Rino said. "But I think Fujita got what he came for."

Mr. Sato nodded. "Please come inside. We must talk."

The old man's one-room cottage was a mess of broken furniture, shattered pottery, and scattered papers. Rino moved to straighten things up, but Mr. Sato held up his hand to stop her.

"There is no time," he said. He took a seat on the one wooden chair that had not been destroyed in the fight. Hiro and the others gathered around Mr. Sato, waiting for the teacher to tell his story.

"All of you know me as Sato," he began. "But my real name is . . . Okuno."

Hiro heard his mother gasp. He had heard the name before, in the old stories. Okuno was supposed to be the most powerful ninja in Kenkoro—even more powerful than Fujita. But Okuno was a hero who traveled from village to village, helping those in trouble. Could old Mr. Sato and Okuno really be one and the same?

"Do you expect us to believe that?" Kazuki asked rudely. "You're too old to be Okuno."

The old man leapt across the table so quickly that Hiro didn't even see him move. One moment, he was sitting in his chair, and the next, he was standing behind Kazuki with his arm around Kazuki's neck in a choke hold.

"The art of disguise is one of the most important lessons in ninja training," Okuno said, as Kazuki struggled to get out of his grasp. "But perhaps you were not paying attention. I disguised myself as a frail old man and came to this village because I had an important secret to guard."

Okuno released his grasp.

Red-faced, Kazuki rubbed his neck. "Sorry," he said.

"I accept your apology," Okuno said.

"What secret were you guarding?" Hiro asked.

"It is the secret you hold in your hands," Okuno said, motioning toward him.

Hiro placed the torn scroll pieces on the table.

"They look like pieces of maps," Kenta remarked.

"They are," Okuno said. "These maps reveal the locations of two of the most powerful magical talismans ever created: the Amulet of the Moon and the Amulet of the Sun."

Rino and Yuto looked at each other. Hiro had never seen his parents look so grim.

"So that's what Fujita was after," Yuto said. "He wants the power for himself."

Okuno nodded. "Yes. Individually, the amulets are extremely powerful. Together, their power is unstoppable. Ages ago, it was determined that they should be separated, hidden in two secret locations, so that their power could never be abused."

"How did you get the scrolls?" Hiro asked.

"The scrolls were hidden in a temple on a small island for a long, long time," Okuno explained. "Then Fujita learned of them, and began to search for them. The monks at the temple sent for me and asked me to guard them. When I arrived, Fujita and his men were attacking. I fought them off and escaped with the scrolls. But I knew Fujita would not stop until he found me."

"So you disguised yourself as Mr. Sato," Rino said.

Okuno smiled wistfully. "I was young then, and

needed to wear a disguise," he said. "Now I truly am an old man. But I am not as frail as I pretend to be."

He looked at Kazuki, his dark eyes twinkling.

Hiro enjoyed seeing his oldest brother look uncomfortable for a change. But a cold pit of fear was forming in his belly.

"Fujita finally found you," Hiro said.

"He did," Okuno agreed. "I protected this house with charms against intruders, but Fujita broke them. The only charm that held was one I used to prevent animal transformation."

"So that's why I couldn't enter in bear form," Kazuki said. "But it didn't matter. Fujita got the scrolls."

Okuno picked up the scroll pieces on the table. "Incorrect. He only got part of the scrolls, thanks to Hiro."

Hiro blushed. "I'm sorry I couldn't save all of the scrolls."

"You did your best, Hiro, and you have given us

a valuable gift: time," Okuno said. "Fujita will need time to figure out the exact location of the amulets. I must stay here to protect the village in case he returns. But you can use that time to retrieve the amulets first. The Hinata family must do this. It is your destiny."

He looked directly at Yuto, who nodded solemnly. Hiro didn't understand what Okuno meant. As far as he knew, the only destiny his family had was to protect their small village.

"How will we know where to go, if the scrolls are torn?" Kenta asked.

"I have memorized both locations," Okuno told them. "The Amulet of the Moon is closest to the village. Fujita will most likely seek that out first."

"We will leave at first light," Rino said.

"Fujita will know we will try to get the amulets first," Okuno warned. "You may be followed."

"We will keep our eyes and ears open," Yuto promised.

Kazuki suddenly jumped up, slamming his fist on the table. He pointed to the open window.

"Someone is watching us now!"

Chapter Five

Kazuki sprang across the room and reached through the open window.

"Hey!" Yoshi cried out as Kazuki pulled him into the room.

"Kazuki! Put him down!" Rino scolded.

Kazuki dropped Yoshi, who landed on the floor with a thud.

"You didn't have to do that," Yoshi protested. "We heard the alarms, and then we heard a bunch of noise coming from our teacher's house."

"We?" Kazuki asked.

Aya calmly walked through the front door. "We heard everything, sensei," she said, bowing to Okuno. "Yoshi and I want to help."

Rino looked worried. "It's going to be dangerous. I'm not even sure Hiro should make the journey."

"Mom, no!" Hiro cried out in protest. This was his first important task as a ninja. He couldn't bear the thought of staying home.

"We don't need you pipsqueaks. We can handle this," Kazuki said.

Okuno stroked his long white beard thoughtfully. "It is unwise to underestimate Fujita. Aya, Yoshi, and Hiro are young. But they are skilled. If you do not take them, I fear you will regret it."

"All right!" Hiro and Yoshi shouted together. Aya's green eyes gleamed with excitement.

"I will talk to each of your parents now," Rino said. "Boys, help your father. We will need supplies for the journey."

She turned to Okuno. "Where are we going?"

Okuno straightened out one of the scroll pieces. The torn map showed part of a long mountain chain.

"Deep beneath the Kagetsu Mountains is an underground cavern," he explained. "The Amulet of the Moon was placed there, but it is heavily guarded."

"Guarded by warriors?" Hiro asked.

Okuno shrugged. "I do not know. You must be prepared for anything. The wise ones took great precautions to make sure the amulet would not fall into the wrong hands."

"We will make sure that does not happen," Yuto said solemnly.

"You must," Okuno said. "If you fail, it will mean the end of all we know."

Okuno's ominous words haunted Hiro as he helped his father and brothers prepare for the journey. Hiro filled his pack with a bedroll, his bowl and cup, and a jug of clean water. Yuto gathered the rest of the supplies and divided them among the packs. Hiro carried a bag of rice and a satchel of dried fish.

The first rays of the sun were just peeking over the mountaintops by the time they were ready. Hiro hoisted the pack onto his back. To keep the packs light, they had taken only what was necessary. This would allow them to travel more quickly.

Hiro and his family marched silently through the village in the dim light. Yoshi and Aya waited for them at the start of the path. Yoshi was hopping up and down with excitement.

"I can't believe we're going!" he said, running up to Hiro. "When do you think we'll get to the cavern?"

"Okuno told my parents how to get there," Hiro replied. "My mom said it would take two days."

"Two days!" Yoshi said. "I could transform into a rabbit. I'd get there a lot faster."

"Then somebody would have to carry your pack," Aya said dryly. "And I'm not going to do that."

"Who needs a pack?" Yoshi asked. "I'll eat

wildflowers. I'll sleep in a hole in the ground. I'll drink from rain puddles."

Aya shook her head. "Don't you know anything?" she asked. "If you stay in your animal form too long, you'll stay that way forever."

Yoshi considered this. "So what?" he said finally. "That wouldn't be so bad. I wouldn't have to milk the goats anymore. Do you know what a barn full of goats smells like?" He shuddered comically.

"Well, I don't think I would like being a snake all the time," Aya said. She made a face. "I'd have to eat mice and rats for the rest of my life. Yuck!"

Hiro stared down at his sandals and kicked a stone in the path. He badly wanted to join in the conversation, but he had nothing to say. Aya noticed his expression.

"Don't worry, Hiro," she said. "I'm sure you'll learn to change soon."

"You said that yesterday," Hiro said. "So did my mom. But until it happens, I won't believe it."

They walked on in silence for a while. Kenta, who

never did anything slowly, walked on ahead of the group. Hiro's parents trailed behind him, talking in hushed whispers. Kazuki insisted on taking up the rear so he could watch for threats from behind.

"You heard Okuno," Kazuki said. "We need to be ready for anything."

Hiro was glad to have Aya and Yoshi's company. He had known both his friends since they were very small. Unlike Hiro, they didn't come from ninja families. Yoshi's parents kept goats, and Aya's mother was the most skilled weaver in the village. Rino and Yuto had handpicked the two of them for ninja training when they were just five years old.

The day was shaping up to be one of those beautiful spring days that made you forget all about the harsh chill of winter. White, puffy clouds floated in the blue sky. The valley leading to the Kagetsu Mountains was bursting with new life. Fresh green grass felt soft beneath their feet. Tiny white flowers dotted the landscape, creeping up the rocky mountainsides on either side of them.

Lines of scraggly pines grew on the valley's edges. Hiro heard a loud caw and saw a group of black crows perched in the branches.

"I wonder what other animals live in these mountains," he said out loud. "I've never been this far outside the village."

"I came this way once, when we went to visit my grandmother," Yoshi said. "We saw some mountain goats, but that was about it."

As they walked, a beam of sunlight glinted off of a charm hanging around Hiro's neck. Aya glanced at it.

"You know, I always wondered," she said. "Everyone in your family wears that charm. It's beautiful. Does it mean something special?"

Hiro looked down at the charm, which was threaded on a leather cord. The silver circle was engraved with a symbol of the moon and sun intertwined. He'd been wearing it since he was a baby.

"It's the symbol of our family," Hiro explained.

"We always wear them. I guess I never thought about it before."

"If our family had a symbol, it would be a goat," Yoshi joked.

They came to the end of the valley. The path became a narrow pass between two mountains. They all stopped. Once they entered the pass, they would be vulnerable to attack from all sides.

"I'll run up ahead and scout it out," Kenta offered. Yuto nodded, and Kenta quickly transformed into a wolf with blue-gray fur. "I'll be back," he promised.

Hiro took a drink from his jug of water while they waited for Kenta. His brother returned a few minutes later in human form.

"All clear," he said. "If anyone is waiting for us, they're well hidden."

They headed into the pass. Hiro marveled at the jagged rock walls that rose up on either side of them, streaked with yellow, red, and black. Hiro tried to remember the names of the stones. The

red was sandstone, and the yellow—

Caw! Caw!

Five black crows circled overhead. Were they the same crows from the valley? Hiro wondered.

The crows circled lower and lower. They set down on a rock ledge overhanging the path up ahead. Hiro suddenly realized what was happening.

"Stop!" he yelled. "They're Fujita's men!"

Hiro's warning came too late. In an instant, the five crows transformed into ninja dressed all in black. They jumped from the ledge and charged forward with lightning speed.

Hiro's heart pounded with fear and excitement. They were under attack!

45

Chapter Six

Kenta immediately transformed into a wolf and sprang at the nearest ninja. With his snarling jaws, he latched on to the ninja's neck and took him down.

Kazuki turned into a big brown bear and swiped at the nearest ninja with massive paws. The man fell backward, then quickly jumped to his feet and aimed a kick at Kazuki. The angry bear roared and batted him away once more.

A flash of orange zipped past Hiro as his father, in his tiger form, pounced on one of the ninja.

Hiro's mother jumped up, spun around, and delivered a hard, powerful kick to the fourth man. He flew backward and hit the ground with a thud.

As the ninja got back on his feet, another charged Rino from behind.

"Looks like there's one left for us," Aya said.

Hiro nodded. "I got it!"

He quickly scrambled up to a ridge in the side of the mountain. Down below, Yoshi ran up to the ninja and aimed a blow right at his stomach. The thug kicked Yoshi's hand away before he could strike.

Hiro jumped down from the ridge, tackling the ninja from above. They both hit the ground hard. Hiro knew he wasn't strong enough to keep the larger man from getting up. Then he heard a whirring sound. A small silver throwing knife whizzed past him. The knife sliced through the man's black shirt, pinning him to the ground.

Hiro grinned at Aya. "Nice aim!"

The easily beaten ninja knew this was a battle he and his gang couldn't win. All five transformed back into crows and broke away, flying over the mountaintops.

Caw! Caw! Caw!

"That was awesome!" Yoshi cheered. "We completely wiped the ground with those guys!"

Hiro's heart was still pounding. He hadn't been afraid to fight, like he was back in Mr. Sato's house. He had done something, and it felt good.

"You all did well," Rino told them. "But I fear this is only the beginning of our troubles."

"What do you mean?" Yoshi asked.

"Fujita had his men follow us," Rino explained. "He knows we are heading to the Kagetsu Mountains. He must have figured out the location of the cavern. That's why he had his men attack us."

Hiro noticed something sparkling on the path. He reached down and picked up a silver token. It was engraved with a picture of a fierce-looking dragon.

"I see," Aya said. "If he didn't know where to

find the amulet yet, those crows would still be following us."

Rino nodded. "We have a head start. But we must hurry."

Hiro handed her the token. "Mom, I found this. Does it mean something?"

Rino's blue eyes clouded. "It is Fujita's mark. A warning of what is to come."

She tossed the token into a clump of weeds. Then she shook her head and forced a smile. "Come. Let's keep moving."

They moved through the mountain pass as quickly as they could. Hiro's neck hurt from staring up at the sky. He kept expecting those crows to come swooping back down on them—the crows, or something worse. He kept picturing the dragon talisman. What kind of message was Fujita sending?

They came through the pass into another valley just as the sun was beginning to set. Yuto suggested they set up camp.

"We need rest to face what lies ahead," he said.

"We'll eat something and sleep—for a few hours, at least."

It felt good to stop moving for a while. Kenta and Kazuki started a fire, while Hiro and Yoshi fetched water from a nearby stream. Rino cooked a pot of rice. It smelled delicious, and Hiro realized how hungry he was.

"That was a great fight back there," Yoshi said, as he dug into his bowl of food. "The way you guys transformed into your animal spirits was amazing."

"Thanks," Kenta said. "Hey, did you and Aya learn how to transform yet? How come you didn't change during the fight?"

"I'm a rabbit," Yoshi said proudly. Kazuki started to laugh, but Rino shot him a warning look. "Rabbits are fast. Good for running, not so good for fighting," Yoshi explained.

"I understand," Rino said. "Not all animal forms are suited for battle. I rarely transform into a crane when I need to fight."

"I guess I could use being a snake in battle, but

I'm not sure how yet," Aya admitted. "I don't want to transform until I'm sure."

"I think Mr. Sato would applaud your patience," Yuto said. "I mean, Okuno."

"Dad, what did Okuno mean when he said finding the amulets was our destiny?" Hiro blurted out. The question had been lurking in the back of his mind all day. Now that they were getting closer to their goal, he wanted to know the answer.

Rino and Yuto exchanged glances. After a moment, Rino gave her husband a nod.

"It's about time you all knew," Yuto said, sighing. "It's all a little hard to believe, actually."

"I'll believe you," Hiro promised.

Yuto put down his bowl and settled back on his elbows. The light from the flames of the fire danced on his face, reminding Hiro of his father's tiger stripes.

"It all began ages ago," he explained. "Two families were at war. The war had raged for so long that nobody could remember how it started.

But that did not matter. Each family wanted power over the other.

"The Hinata family sent their oldest son, Daichi, to be trained by the greatest sorcerers in the world when he was very young," Yuto went on. "Without knowing this, the Gekkani family sent their oldest daughter, Mai. The two children grew up with the sorcerers, studying the oldest forms of magic. When they turned sixteen, the two children were returned to their families."

"Gekkani—that's Mom's family name," Kenta interrupted.

"Yes," Rino said. "That girl was my ancestor."

"Back home, each used the knowledge they had learned to create an amulet that would give their family special power," Yuto explained. "Daichi created the Amulet of the Sun. Mai created the Amulet of the Moon. Each amulet embodies the energy of these celestial bodies. The power of the amulets can be used to create, or to destroy. When Daichi and Mai created the amulets, they did not know that their families each wanted the power to destroy the other."

"What happened when they learned the truth?" Aya asked.

"Daichi and Mai had become good friends when they trained together. They only wanted peace between their families. So they turned the amulets over to a group of monks to be hidden away forever," Yuto said. "The stories do not say what happened to Daichi and Mai. The family war waged on for a few more years, and then slowly quieted down."

"When your father and I married, we united the Hinata and Gekkani families for the first time," Rino explained. "Only a member of the Hinata family can wield the Amulet of the Sun. And only a member of the Gekkani family can wield the Amulet of the Moon. That is our destiny."

Hiro looked down at the charm around his neck. The sun and the moon combined—it made sense now. When his parents married, it brought together the two families. They brought together the sun and the moon.

"And what about us?" Hiro asked after a moment. "Kenta, Kazuki, and I. We're both Hinata and Gekkani, aren't we?"

"Your father and I have discussed that," Rino said. "Kenta and Kazuki have the eyes of the Gekkani. You have your father's eyes—the eyes of the Hinata. Your father and I will wield the amulets. But if anything happens to us, we believe your brothers can carry the Amulet of the Moon, and you can carry the Amulet of the Sun. We hope this is true. No other hand may touch the amulets. "

If anything happens to us. The words chilled Hiro. But he had one more question.

"What about Fujita?" Hiro asked. "What will happen if he tries to touch the amulets? He is not a Hinata or a Gekkani."

"He may not know this rule," Yuto said. "Or he may have created a charm that will allow him to carry them. His magic has grown very powerful.

But we do not know for sure."

"Enough stories," Rino said, standing up. "Let's wash out our bowls in the stream. We must sleep while we can."

Chapter Seven

A crescent-shaped moon gleamed brightly in the sky as they laid out their bedrolls for the night. Hiro fell asleep easily. It was still dark when Rino woke him up a few hours later.

"Time to go," she said, brushing his hair from his forehead.

Hiro groaned softly. He felt like he could sleep for hours and hours, but he didn't complain. He was a ninja now, not a little kid.

"Is it time to wake up already?" Yoshi asked, yawning. "Can't we just sleep a little more?"

Kenta pulled the bedroll out from under him. "We've got to get to the amulet before Fujita does. I've heard he doesn't need to sleep or eat. He lives on pure energy."

"And I've heard he's got eyes in the back of his head," Yoshi added, as he hopped to his feet.

"Those are just stories," Rino said, as she filled up her pack. "Most of them aren't true."

"Most of them?" Hiro asked curiously.

"Never mind," Rino said quickly. "If we get to the amulet soon, we won't have to worry about Fujita."

The new moon wasn't bright enough to light their way, so they lit torches from the fire before putting it out. Then they headed down the trail again.

Walking in the dark was tricky. The torchlight cast strange shadows around them. Hiro imagined one of Fujita's ninja lurking in each one of them. He expected to see those strange, red eyes glowing in the darkness at any moment.

By the time the fire of their torches died out, the sun was rising once again. They emerged into the foothills of the Kagetsu Mountains just as dawn broke. The tall mountain peaks looked blue in the morning sunlight. Around them, brown rabbits munched on yellow flowers that grew like weeds on the grassy slopes.

"Be careful," Kazuki called out. "Those could be Fujita's men."

Hiro shook his head. "Right. He sent an army of rabbits to defeat us."

"Hey!" Yoshi cried out, offended. "Rabbits can be tough."

He balled his hands into fists and bounced toward Hiro, pretending to box him. Hiro moved his hands in front of his face to protect himself. Yoshi aimed a pretend punch, and Hiro did a backward somersault and flopped onto the grass.

"Beaten by a rabbit!" Hiro cried.

Yoshi raised his arms in the air, victorious. "Don't mess with me! I am one bad bunny!"

Hiro laughed and jumped up, doing a quick headstand before getting to his feet. They walked on. Hiro felt his mother's hand on his shoulder.

"It's good to see you having fun," Rino told him. "This last year you've been training so hard. I never see you smile anymore."

"Being a ninja is serious," Hiro said. "I want to be a good one."

"I know," Rino said. "But to be the best ninja you can, you still must be Hiro."

"What do you mean? I *am* Hiro!" he said.

Rino patted his head. "Yes, you are."

Before he could figure out what she meant by that, his mother walked on ahead of him. She moved so smoothly, Hiro sometimes wondered if her feet really touched the ground.

They walked a little farther and came upon a tall pine tree. Yuto held up his hand.

"Okuno said the cavern would be here."

They headed toward the base of the mountain. Sure enough, there was a small hole carved into the rock.

"This must be it," Yuto said.

Kazuki held up his torch, ready to light it, but Rino stopped him.

"If Fujita is waiting for us, we'll be spotted," she said. "We'll have to adjust to the darkness."

"No problem," Kenta said. He transformed into his wolf form. "Gotta love that night vision."

Yuto transformed into a tiger. Hiro had seen his father in tiger form only a few times. His body was thick and powerful, with sharp claws. He had a big, shaggy head and large jaws. Hiro would have been afraid, but his father's kind eyes shone from the tiger's face.

"Kenta and I will lead the way," he said.

The wolf and tiger easily slipped through the entrance. Rino went next, with Aya, Yoshi, and Hiro following her. Hiro heard a grunt behind him as Kazuki struggled to fit through the small opening.

"You okay there, Kazuki?" Hiro asked.

"Watch it, Hiro," Kazuki said. "Or I'll turn into a bear right now and squash you."

"He doesn't need to turn into a bear to do that," Yoshi whispered, and Hiro stifled a laugh.

But this was no time to make jokes. They made their way inside a dark tunnel with a low ceiling. Kazuki had to crouch down as they walked. Hiro didn't have night vision, but his eyes slowly adjusted. He could see Yoshi's white hair in front of him.

The tunnel soon opened up into a small room.

"Stop!" Yuto hissed. "Okuno said the amulet was guarded. He was right."

Hiro gently pushed Yoshi aside, straining to see. On the other side of the room was a door carved into the stone. There was a lock underneath the door handle. To the left of the door hung a golden key that gleamed in the darkness.

A strange creature slept beneath the key, snoring. The creature had a body as large as a lion's, covered with matted reddish-brown fur. Each of its three big, round heads had the snout of a dog and a curly mane like a lion's. The mouths opened and closed as the dog yawned, revealing white, razor-sharp teeth.

Yuto led them back into the passageway.

"It's a *shisa*," Rino whispered. "A lion dog. But this one has three heads."

"We can fight it," Kazuki said. "I'll transform."

Rino shook her head. "It's too dangerous."

"But we have to get that key," Kazuki pointed out.

"If we're quiet, we could sneak past it and get the key," Hiro suggested.

"None of us is quiet enough to do that," Yuto said. "Not even your mother."

"I'm quiet enough," Aya said.

"What can you do?" Kazuki asked.

Aya closed her eyes. Her skin slowly began to turn a pale green. Then shiny scales appeared on her skin. In the next instant, she transformed.

A brilliant green snake slithered across the floor of the cavern. Hiro held his breath as Aya made her way down the passageway.

Slowly and quietly, she glided past the sleeping

shisa. She extended her body upward, slipping her head through the key ring. It slipped down onto her neck.

Aya quickly slithered back to the group, and Rino slid the key from her neck. Then Aya transformed back into her human form. Her skin still glistened a scaly pale green, and she looked exhausted.

"Good work, Aya," Rino said.

Aya smiled proudly. The green of her skin had faded completely now. Rino hurried to the door and put the key in the lock. There was a click as the lock unhinged, and then the door creaked open.

Grrrrrrrrrr!

"Kazuki, is that you?" Kenta whispered. "You really shouldn't—"

The shisa sprang, all three heads snarling and snapping at once. Rino pulled open the door.

"Hurry!" she cried.

Chapter Eight

"Run!" Yuto ordered. "I'll take care of the shisa."

Yuto charged at the three-headed beast, his fangs bared. The tiger slammed into the shisa, knocking it to the ground.

Hiro couldn't move. He wanted to help his father somehow, but what could he do? Then his mother's voice cut through the air.

"Run! We must get the amulet!" Rino shouted. "Hiro, obey your father!"

Hiro knew his mother was right. He turned and ran through the door, leaving the sound of the growling beasts behind him.

They ran as fast as they could through another dark tunnel. The path sloped down steeply as they made their way farther and farther underground, following twists and turns. Finally, Hiro spotted a bright beam of sunlight at the end of the tunnel. But they were deep underground. That didn't make sense.

When they reached the end of the tunnel, Hiro saw where the light was coming from. They emerged into a large cavern with a high ceiling. Hundreds of crystals hung from the ceiling. Each one glowed with soft white light from within.

The cavern was shaped like a circle, and in the center of the circle was a dark pool of water. The glow of the crystals reflected on the water like rays of moonlight.

A round pillar made of polished crystal rose up in the very center of the pool. On top of the pillar sat

a round band of silver adorned with a silver circle.
The light from the glowing crystals illuminated the
wristband, and it gleamed so brightly, Hiro almost
had to look away.

It could only be one thing.

"The Amulet of the Moon," Hiro said out loud. His
voice bounced off of the cavern walls.

"I'm on it," Kenta said. Still in wolf form, he dove
into the pool.

"Be careful, Kenta," Rino warned. "There could
be more traps in the water."

"They're coming!"

Yuto ran into the cavern, human once more. Hiro
was relieved to see his father safe. But Yuto had
bad news.

"Fujita and his men are here," he said. "The
shisa is keeping them busy. But they won't be—"

Three ninja stormed into the cavern, knocking
Yuto down. His head smacked against the hard stone
floor. Kazuki charged at them, but one of the men
somersaulted right over him, landing in the pool.

The ninja transformed into a shark in midair and shot toward Kenta.

"Kenta, get out of the pool now!" Hiro yelled.

Rino held her arms at her sides. The large sleeves of her tunic looked like wings. A soft blue glow enveloped her as she became a crane flying over the pool.

Kazuki was locked in a grip with one of the ninja. Aya was bravely fighting the other one, gracefully dodging his blows. Next to her, Yoshi transformed into a rabbit and quickly hopped off around the pool.

Maybe he's scared, Hiro guessed. *I don't blame him.*

Then he remembered Kenta. His brother was swimming as fast as he could to the edge of the pool. The shark's head rose out of the water, and his jaws opened wide, ready to chomp Kenta's tail.

Hiro reached out and grabbed his brother's paw, helping to pull him out of the pool. Kenta transformed and sat up, coughing and spitting out water.

At the center of the pool, Rino picked up the

moon amulet in her long, slim beak. She had done it!

Then the ninja fighting Kazuki broke away, transforming into a huge eagle. He soared after Rino. She flew up to the high ceiling of the cavern, and the eagle followed, reaching out with his claws.

Hiro raced around the pool. There had to be some way to help his mother. The eagle lashed out again, and he heard Rino cry out.

"Mom, no!" Hiro yelled.

Chapter Nine

Kenta transformed back into a wolf and jumped clear across the pool, but he couldn't reach the eagle.

Hiro jumped up, trying to reach the glowing crystals. There had to be some way to swing up there and help his mom. He was a good climber, but the crystals were just too high.

If I were a monkey I could get up there! Hiro thought. He jumped again with all his might . . .

. . . and transformed in midair! A strange
sensation filled him as the change took over his
body. It took less than a second, but each part of
the transformation seemed as if it was happening
in slow motion. Coarse hair sprouted all over his
body. A long tail grew from the base of his spine.

Hiro didn't need to look in a mirror to know what
he was. He could feel it.

He was a monkey.

And that's exactly what he needed to be. He

swung from crystal to crystal until he reached the
eagle. Then he reached out with one strong foot
and kicked the eagle in the abdomen.

The eagle let out a cry and faltered, losing
its grip on Rino. Kazuki reached up and swatted
down the bird with a massive bear paw. The eagle
transformed back into a ninja as it hit the floor, and
Kazuki held him down with one big foot.

Rino floated to the ground and transformed. She
slipped the silver band onto her wrist.

A blinding blue glow shone from the amulet. Hiro

swung down to the floor, shielding his eyes. As he hit the ground, he unwillingly transformed back into a human.

Guess I need to get used to this, Hiro realized.

Rino closed her eyes, and the glow slowly faded.

"I think I can control it," she said.

Aya and Kenta walked over, each of them holding one of Yuto's arms. Hiro's dad looked dazed.

"I'll be all right," he said, letting go to stand on his own. "We need to get out of here, but we're in for another fight. Fujita is out there somewhere."

Yoshi came hopping up. "I figured we'd need to find another way out. And rabbits are good at getting in and out of tunnels!" he said. His nose twitched as he talked. "I found one that leads out of here on the other side of the pool. Follow me and I'll show you."

Before they could follow, a thunderous roar filled the cavern. The massive head of a dragon emerged from the tunnel. Glistening purple scales covered its skin. Its huge open mouth looked large enough to swallow them all in one gulp. For a second, Hiro thought it might be another guardian of the amulet, but then the dragon's eyes began to glow a deep, dark red.

Horror swept through Hiro's body as he realized the truth. The dragon was Fujita, transformed!

An orange glow burned in the dragon's throat.

"Everybody run!" Rino yelled. "Follow Yoshi!"

Chapter Ten

They followed the rabbit around the pool to the back of the cavern. A blazing hot fireball shot from the dragon's mouth. Hiro ducked into the tunnel Yoshi had found just in time. He could feel the heat from the blast on his back.

Yuto and Kenta had transformed into tiger and wolf so they could run faster. Hiro heard the roar of the dragon as it entered the tunnel behind them. They didn't have much time.

His thoughts raced as he charged ahead.

Fujita's a dragon! Who can transform into a dragon? He'd never heard of anything like it before. Suddenly transforming into a monkey didn't seem like such a big deal.

A shaft of sunlight appeared ahead of them, and they all raced out into the open. Fujita was right behind them. He opened his wide mouth again, ready to shoot another fireball.

Rino stopped and turned to face him. She thrust out her left arm. The silver Moon Amulet glinted in the sunlight.

"BACK!" she screamed, as a blinding streak of blue light shone from the amulet. The light struck Fujita, and the dragon let out a roar of pain, shrinking away from them.

Rino took a step closer. The light from the amulet grew more powerful every moment. Rino's eyes gleamed as the power surged through her body like ocean waves during a storm. Fujita backed up into the tunnel.

Rino lowered her arm, and the light faded. She collapsed in a heap on the ground. Yuto transformed into his human form and ran to her side.

"Are you all right?" he asked.

She nodded and slowly rose to her feet. "Just a little weak. I could feel it connecting to the energy inside me. I think it derives its power from the wearer."

"Is Fujita gone?" Hiro asked.

Yuto looked back at where the dragon had loomed. "For now," Yuto answered. "But he will be back. He will try to find a way to take the Amulet of the Moon from us. And he still searches for the Amulet of the Sun."

"Then we should get out of here," Kenta said.

They headed off down the sloping hills. Hiro hung behind, lost in thought.

Everything seemed so unreal. They had the amulet, they'd defeated Fujita, but things seemed more dangerous than ever. And no one had even mentioned that Hiro had transformed into a monkey.

Rino stopped and waited for Hiro to catch up. She put an arm on his shoulder.

"How are you doing, Hiro?" she asked.

"I'm okay," he replied. "You know, you were really awesome back there."

"We were all awesome," Rino said, smiling. "Especially you, Hiro. You transformed just in time to help me."

"Yeah, into a monkey," Kazuki snorted. "Ooh, really scary."

"Hey, I think monkeys are cool," Kenta said. But he couldn't resist teasing his little brother. "Those extra-long arms come in handy when you need to scratch your butt."

For once, the teasing didn't bother Hiro. He grinned.

"Maybe," he said. "But I can also do this."

Hiro did a backflip, then another. On his third flip, he launched himself into the air and transformed just in time to grab on to a tree branch.

"See ya later!" he called down. He swung to the next branch, and then to the next tree. It felt almost like flying.

Yoshi turned into a rabbit and hopped beneath him. "No fair! Wait up!"

Aya folded her arms, annoyed. "Have fun without me. You know snakes can't jump."

Hiro laughed and swung to the next tree. They might be headed into danger, but for now, for just a little while, he could play. He swung forward, somersaulted in the air, and grabbed the next branch with a loud cry.

"Monkey power!"

HIRO'S WORLD

**Hiro's Quest is a work of fantasy, but
it is based on some real ideas
and elements from Japan and other places
around the world.**

Glossary

amulet an object, usually a piece of jewelry, with special powers. People traditionally wore amulets to protect themselves from evil.

Kenkoro the magical kingdom where Hiro lives

ninja a class of warriors who learned martial arts and were known for their ability to attack silently and swiftly

quest a long and difficult search

sensei a Japanese word meaning "teacher"

scroll a sheet of paper with writing on it that can be rolled up

shisa a guardian animal that is half lion, half dog. Statues of shisa can be found on the rooftops or gates of Japanese homes to protect them from evil spirits. The Japanese shisa is related to a Chinese lion dog called a "fu dog."

sorcerer someone who practices magic, such as a wizard or magician

About the Animal Spirits

In Hiro's world, each ninja has an animal spirit and can transform into that animal at will. When a ninja is in human form, the traits of his or her animal spirit are apparent in the way he or she looks or acts.

Here's a guide to some of the animal spirits in this book. Which of these animal spirits are you most like?

bear A ninja with a bear spirit is usually very big and strong. Bear ninja are not as agile as other ninja, but they make up for it with sheer power. Bears can be lazy, and they love to sleep. But when danger threatens someone they care about, bear ninja will fight back ferociously.

crane These waterbirds have long legs and long necks, so crane ninja are usually tall, thin, and graceful. They're good-looking, too—cranes are known for their beauty. Crane ninja are peace-loving, but they are skilled in the martial arts and will not hesitate to do battle when the cause is just.

dragon Dragon ninja have fiery personalities and often act without thinking. Dragons are magical creatures, and few ninja have the ability to transform into them. The dragon spirit wields incredible power. Dragon ninja come in different shapes and sizes, but you can usually tell who they are by their eyes, which are as dark as night and glisten like rubies.

monkey Ninja who are adept at things like gymnastics and climbing often have monkey spirits inside them. Monkey ninja are curious and playful. Some animal types prefer being alone, but monkey ninja are always happiest when they're around friends and family. Monkey types can be short or tall, but they're always in good shape.

rabbit Rabbit ninja are impatient and very rarely stand still. They're usually short and can run very fast. Rabbit ninja make great guards because they have a sixth sense that can detect when danger is near. These ninja are fun to be around—if you can keep up with them.

snake These ninja move silently and gracefully. Snake ninja are intelligent and skilled at plotting out their moves in battle. They can strike swiftly, without warning, surprising the enemy. Snake ninja might seem a little cold or standoffish but will become loyal friends with those they trust. Snake ninja often have deep green eyes.

tiger A tiger is one of nature's fiercest predators, and tiger ninja are hard to beat in battle. In their human form, they're usually very muscular, strong, and fast. Family is extremely important to tiger ninja. Tiger ninja use keen sight and smell to hunt.

wolf Wolf ninja use speed and tireless energy to track prey for miles. Lean and unkempt, wolf ninja are fast and don't get tired easily. Like the tiger, wolf ninja have excellent senses of sight and smell.

Into the Fire

Hiro and his family successfully prevented **evil warlord Fujita** from getting his hands on the Amulet of the Moon. But they must also protect the Amulet of the Sun from the dark ninja's grasp. And with a **gang of stealthy ninjas on the attack**, Hiro knows it will not be easy to get to the sacred talisman before Fujita does. He'll have to use **all of his ninja skills**—and his newfound monkey spirit—to help defeat Fujita once and for all. **Even when it means descending into the depths of a deadly volcano . . .**